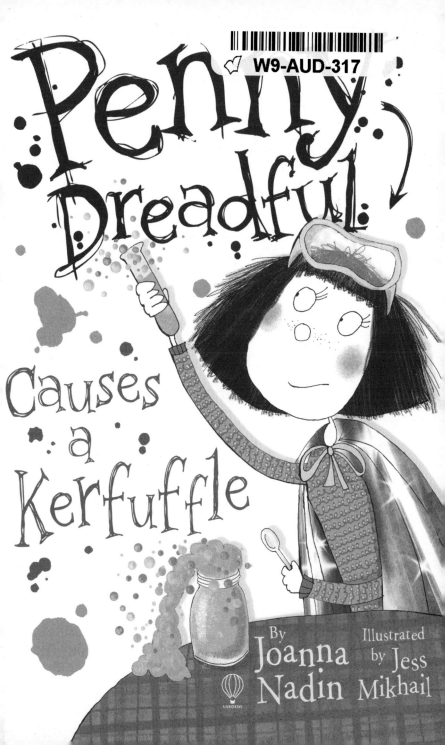

Penny Dreadful

Causes a Kerfuffle

By Joanna Nadin

Illustrated by Jess Mikhail

Contents

Penny Dreadful
and the New Girl
page 89

Penny Dreadful's
Top **5** Tips for Survival
page 132

Penny Dreadful

Does Her Best

My name
is not actually
Penny Dreadful. It is Penelope Jones.

The "Dreadful" part is my dad's **JOKE**. I know it

is a joke because every time he says it he laughs

like a honking goose. But I do not see the funny

side. Plus it is not even true that I am dreadful.

It is like Gran says, i.e. that I am a **MAGNET FOR DISASTER**. Mom says if Gran kept a better eye on me in the first place instead of on Judge Janet at 2pm on Crime 21 then I might not be quite so magnetic. But Gran says if Mom wasn't so busy answering phones for Dr. Cement, who is her boss and who has bulgy eyes like hard-boiled eggs (which is why everyone calls him Dr. Bugeye), and Dad wasn't so busy solving crises at the council, then they would be able to solve some crises at 73 Rollins Road, i.e. our house. So you see it is completely not my fault.

★ ☆ ✦ ✹

For instance it is completely not my fault that right now I am utterly bluish all over, and so is my best friend Cosmo Moon Webster, and so is my sister Daisy's swan outfit, and so is our best tablecloth. It is probably definitely the fault of Mr. Schumann, our principal, who is most often saying things like "Penelope Jones, for the last time spoons are for **EATING WITH** not **BALANCING ON YOUR NOSE**." And it is especially annoying because I was **ONLY TRYING TO HELP**. So here is what happened.

On Friday, Bridget Grimes, who is the best

student and Mr. Schumann's favorite, is not wearing the school uniform (which is red top, gray bottoms, white socks and black shoes that must be **SENSIBLE**) and Miss Patterson, who is our teacher and very tall and thin like a beanpole, does not **EVEN** say anything to her. And I do not think this is fair, because Cosmo Moon Webster **DOES** get in trouble because he is wearing a Jedi outfit, because his mom (who is called Sunflower, even though her real name is Barbara) believes in **FREEDOM** and **SELF-EXPRESSION**. And I get in trouble for wearing rain boots, which is not because my mom believes in **FREEDOM** and **SELF-EXPRESSION**, it is because one of my shoes is down the drain after I was testing to see if it fit through the gaps in the drain cover and it turns out it does, which I tell Miss Patterson.

And I also tell her that the boots are very **SENSIBLE**, especially if it rains, but she does not agree. And Bridget Grimes, who mostly says annoying things like "I would not do that if I were you, Penelope Jones," says something else which is very annoying, which is:

I **AM** in **UNIFORM** anyway, it is a **BROWNIE** uniform, and Mr. Schumann says I can wear it in assembly and tell everyone about my badges.

And this is completely true, because in assembly Mr. Schumann makes Bridget Grimes stand up and show everyone her badges, and she has one for agility and one for science investigating and one for being a friend to the animals, even though I have seen her step on a worm. Which I am trying to tell Mr. Schumann about by sticking my hand up and saying "Me, me," and also Cosmo is wanting to say something and is sticking his hand up and saying "Me, me," but it is not about Bridget, it is about Henry Potts (who is Cosmo's mortal enemy and who is poking him with a ruler).

But Mr. Schumann cannot seem to see me and Cosmo even though we are not wearing capes of invisibility and Cosmo is actually wearing the Jedi outfit (which is very **VISIBLE**), because he is still talking and what he is saying is that being a **BROWNIE** is all about **DOING YOUR BEST** and **TRYING TO HELP**

without expecting a thank you back. And then he also says,

Penelope Jones and Cosmo Moon Webster, I am **SICK AND TIRED** of you creating a **KERFUFFLE** in assembly. That is the fifth time this week, so you will have to spend recess doing some thinking **INSIDE** instead of playing **OUTSIDE**.

So at recess we do our **THINKING**, which is:

1. We would rather be outside because we can see Luke Bruce on the jungle gym and he is upside down and dangling by one leg which is **AMAZING** and we think we would like to try it.

b) Are elves real?

iii) Who would win in a fight between Minimus Mayhem, leader of the Herobots, and a Tyrannosaurus rex?

Which is when Mr. Schumann comes into the classroom and asks us what we are **THINKING**. And I say we are **THINKING** about whether Minimus Mayhem, leader of the Herobots, would beat a Tyrannosaurus rex in a fight if the Tyrannosaurus had rocket-powered boots on. Which Mr. Schumann says is not the sort of **THINKING** he was **THINKING** about and in fact we should be **THINKING** about what we can learn from Bridget Grimes, i.e. **DOING OUR BEST** and **TRYING TO BE HELPFUL**. Which I am not too happy about because normally I do not like learning things from Bridget Grimes, because normally it is things like "If you keep doing that it will get stuck" (which it did). Only I **THINK** I actually want to try **DOING MY BEST** and **TRYING TO HELP**, and so does Cosmo, and so we decide we are going to be **BROWNIES**.

Only Bridget Grimes says Cosmo cannot be a Brownie because he is not a **GIRL** and that I cannot be a Brownie because I am not usually **DOING MY BEST**, I am usually doing things like throwing erasers at Henry Potts. So Cosmo says he will get his mom to have a one-woman sit-in protest to let boys into Brownies (because she is very big on one-woman sit-in protests). And I say I am going to stop throwing erasers at Henry Potts, and I am going to **DO MY BEST** and **TRY TO HELP** instead, and we will both be Brownies before Bridget knows it.

And so for all the rest of the day I do not throw an eraser at Henry Potts and nor does Cosmo, even though Henry throws all sorts of mortal-enemy things at **US**, e.g.:

1. A protractor

b) A pencil with a troll on the end

3. A bottle of glue, which hits Alexander Pringle, who wears age-14 size clothes even though he is nine and who is eating a lemon cupcake, and a piece of cupcake gets stuck and he starts to turn red and so Cosmo **TRIES TO HELP**, i.e. he hits him on the back, and the cupcake flies out again.

And we are utterly **PLEASED AS PUNCH**. But some people are not pleased, e.g. Alexander Pringle, who is still hungry. And Henry Potts, who gets sent to Mr. Schumann and has to write a hundred lines saying *I will not throw things at other children*. And Bridget Grimes, who starts to cry because her hair (which is very long and actually reaches her waist and she is always swishing it and saying "My hair actually reaches my waist, Penelope Jones") has gotten a piece of lemon cupcake stuck in her hair with glue, and Miss Patterson has to cut a piece of it out with craft scissors.

✫ ✩ ✭ ✯

The next day someone else is also utterly not
PLEASED AS PUNCH and it is my mom, because:

1. Dr. Cement is having a crisis with his filing
cabinet because he has lost Mrs.

Nougat and her bunions

somewhere in the Bs

by mistake and Mom

has to go to the office

on her day off.

2. Daisy (who is my big sister and

who is utterly

annoying) is

being doubly

annoying because she

wants to wear her swan

outfit to Lucy B. Finnegan's costume party tonight, only there is chocolate pudding on it from my experiment yesterday.

c) Dad is playing golf and the last time he did that he hit Mr. Butterworth on the head with a ball, who forgot who he was for three hours and especially forgot that he was married to Mrs. Butterworth from the general store, although Dad says that was a good thing and I agree because Mrs. Butterworth has a mustache and a beady eye (which is mostly on me).

So Cosmo says,

Do not fear, Janet, we will come to your rescue and **DO OUR BEST** and **TRY TO HELP**.

Only Mom says she has enough to worry about without me and Cosmo trying to do anything, and also if Cosmo calls her Janet one more time she may well have a conniption fit. (Only we do not know what this is, so we look it up and it is a tantrum for grown-ups and Cosmo decides he **HAS** to witness a conniption fit and will definitely call her Janet again when she gets back from Dr. Cement's.)

And that is when I have my first **BRILLIANT IDEA™** which is that we will **DO OUR BEST** and **TRY TO HELP** but we will do it secretly without expecting a thank you back, which is even more Brownie-like so they will definitely have to let us in for sure even though Cosmo is a boy.

So what we do is we make a list of all the

HELPFUL things we could do around the house, i.e.:

1. Do the dishes because everything is covered in hard, brown, lumpy dried chocolate pudding.

b) Do the laundry, because that is also covered in hard, brown, lumpy dried chocolate pudding, especially Daisy's swan outfit.

c) Feed Barry, who is Gran's cat, and who is right now eating a hard, brown lump of chocolate pudding even though Mom says he must have **CAT FOOD AND CAT FOOD ONLY**.

Only then I remember that I am not allowed to touch the dishwasher for a lot of reasons, so we cannot do number **1**. And Gran says there is no cat food because I used it up yesterday when I was trying to make a model of Krakatoa (which is a very tall volcano, and the exact color of cat food, only I do not think it melts when you pour lava on it, especially if the lava is actually pudding), so we cannot do number **c)**.

But Cosmo says Barry is actually doing the dishes with his tongue so if we let him eat all the pudding in fact we are being **HELPFUL**, which is very true. So we decide we will just do **b)**, which is *Do the laundry*, and I am not banned from the washing machine yet which Mom says is a **MIRACLE** and Dad says is only a matter of time.

So we get all the laundry in the laundry basket and put it in the machine and get the box of laundry detergent and put a lot of that in too (because the pudding is very lumpy and also there are Dad's red socks in there, only they are a little black from the time I used them to put shoe polish on my face when we were pretending to be aliens from Venus). And

then we have an argument because Cosmo
says he will be in charge of the machine knobs
because he is a boy and a week older, and I say
I will be in charge because the machine is in
my kitchen. And then he says,

No I am.

And I say,

No I am.

And then we decide whoever can get a piece of chocolate pudding to stick to the ceiling will be in charge, and it is me because Cosmo's falls onto Gran's head, who is asleep and amazingly it does not wake her up even though it is very hard. And so I put the machine on **HOT** and am feeling extremely **HELPFUL**.

Only then something **NOT AT ALL HELPFUL** happens, which is that bubbles are coming out of the machine like **CRAZY**, which is very unusual because it absolutely **NEVER** happens when Mom does the laundry, which is a shame because it is actually very pretty.

31

Only soon it is also actually very messy and there are bubbles in places bubbles should not be, e.g. halfway up the chair legs. Which is when I have my second **BRILLIANT IDEA™**, which is to **SUCK** up the bubbles with a vacuum cleaner, only Cosmo says vacuum cleaners are not meant for wet things and he knows because Mr. Schumann has told him so and also banned him from ever using the school vacuum cleaner again. But I say our vacuum cleaner is a special one that can suck up water and shampoo carpets because Mom said it would be useful with all the spillages which are not actually my **FAULT**, they are just **ACCIDENTS**.

So we get the special vacuum cleaner and Cosmo says this time he is in charge because he loves to vacuum and also because he has just gotten some pudding to stick to the kitchen window.

And I do not argue, only it turns out that Cosmo may **LOVE** to vacuum but he is not actually **HELPFUL** at vacuuming, because as well as the bubbles he sucks up some things that are not meant to be sucked, e.g.:

1. Four thumbtacks

2. A plastic monkey

c) Some chocolate pudding

And then another **NOT HELPFUL** thing happens, which is that the vacuum cleaner does not seem very happy with the thumbtacks and the monkey and the chocolate pudding and the bubbles inside because there is an explosion and smoke comes out of it, which Cosmo says is excellent and like Krakatoa. But I do not **THINK** Mom will **THINK** so.

And so we decide to stop vacuuming and
to hang the laundry out to dry, only another
NOT HELPFUL thing has happened, which is
that a lot of the laundry is not the color it was
when it went in, i.e. it has
SOMEHOW turned **PINK**.

And then we are utterly **DISCOMBOBULATED** because Dad does not like wearing pink shirts and also because Daisy says pink is her worst color and that she would **RATHER PERISH** than ever wear it and so would Lucy B. Finnegan. Cosmo says if Daisy did perish I would get her bedroom and her microphone and her collection of plastic zoo animals, and I **THINK** this is true, but I also **THINK** this is not very **HELPFUL** and that we will definitely not be allowed into Brownies. So then Cosmo has his

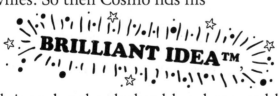

which is to dye the clothes blue, because blue is Daisy's third-best color after yellow, and sparkle, and he knows how to dye things because

Sunflower has dyed all their sheets purple because of the **FREEDOM** and **SELF-EXPRESSION**. Only I say that Mom is not quite so big on **FREEDOM** and **SELF-EXPRESSION** so we do not have any dye, and so we are racking our brains to think of where to get some when Cosmo has another **BRILLIANT IDEA™**, which is that ink is almost exactly like dye and so we can use that instead. And we do definitely have a lot of ink because of the time I knocked over a bottle of grape soda in the general store and Mrs. Butterworth saw it with her beady eye and said Dad would have to pay for the damaged goods, which was eleven Get Well Soon cards, two Famous Castles calendars, and seven bottles of ink.

And so we get the blue ink and the pink laundry and we take it all upstairs to the bathtub and we fill it with water and put everything in. And it is **COMPLETELY** amazing because almost immediately everything changes color, including Dad's shirts and the swan outfit and the best tablecloth, only they are not blue, they are a sort of purplish color, but I say that is okay because purplish is Daisy's fifth-best color and she will not **PERISH**. And we are swirling the ink around the bathtub like **CRAZY**, which is when we notice that our hands have changed color too. And then I have my next **BRILLIANT IDEA™**, which is to get in the bathtub because then we

will definitely look like aliens from Venus and
Mom will not be upset about shoe polish on socks.

And so we do. We get completely in the
bathtub in our clothes and are saying mostly
things like,

> Greetings from Venus,
> take me to your leader...

(which is what aliens sound like) when there is
another sound from downstairs, which I think
could be an alien or it could be Mom because
the sound is a scream sort of sound. And then
I know it is not aliens because the next sound is,

Penelope Jones,
get down here this
INSTANT!

And I do not think
aliens know my
name yet.

So we do go downstairs and the voice is definitely my mom who says she has already **HAD IT UP TO HERE** because of several things, i.e.:

1. That she has spent all morning looking for Mrs. Nougat's bunions **ONLY** to find they are filed under F for **FEET**.

2. That Dad has hit **HIMSELF** on the head with a golf ball and has forgotten how to drive and what his name is, so she has had to pick him up from the golf club.

c) That Daisy and Lucy B. Finnegan have decided they are **NOT** going to be swans **AFTER ALL**, they are going to be rock stars, which is another costume **ENTIRELY**.

So she is **DEFINITELY** not in the mood to come home and find that there are **BUBBLES** where **BUBBLES** should not be, that the vacuum cleaner will not vacuum any more, and that me and Cosmo Moon Webster have turned **BLUE**.

45

And Dad is not in
the mood for anything
because he is not
even sure he lives
here any more.

And Daisy is not
in the mood to find her
swan outfit all blue and
the plastic monkey all
melted and black and says,

It is all your fault,
Penelope Jones, you are
such a complete **MORON**.

And I say it is not my fault, I was only **DOING MY BEST** and trying to be **HELPFUL** so that I can join Brownies and wear my uniform to assembly like Bridget Grimes and get a badge for agility and one for being a friend to the animals. Only then Mom says that I **CANNOT** join Brownies even if I am a friend to the

animals, because it meets at the recreation center and I am not allowed in the recreation center for another two months because of the time I accidentally let

Mrs. Jubilee's chickens into the kitchen, but it was only because they looked cold. So then I am not in the mood for anything at all, especially not being **HELPFUL** or **DOING MY BEST**. Which Mom says is frankly a relief.

But **SOMEONE** is in the mood, and that is Cosmo Moon Webster. Because he says Mom has definitely had a conniption fit and he didn't even have to call her **JANET**.

Penny Dreadful

and the Secret Ingredient

Sometimes I do not
like being Penelope Jones,
and absolutely wish I was Cosmo Moon
Webster, who is my best
friend (even though
he is a week older
than me and a
boy). This is
because of
several things:

1. He does not have to wear a skirt, not **EVER**, unless he chooses. Which he did once, to school, because his mom Sunflower (who is actually named Barbara) believes in **FREEDOM** and **SELF-EXPRESSION** and wrote a note to Mr. Schumann our principal to tell him so.

2) He can touch his nose with the tip of his tongue and I have practiced for two hours and I still cannot do it, not even **CLOSE**.

iii. He is an **ONLY** child, i.e. he does not have a big sister.

Cosmo says actually in fact he would like a big sister because it would be nice to have someone to play war or have a beetle race with, because right now he is very **INTO** beetle races.

But I do not think he would like to have my big sister, i.e. Daisy Jones, because:

a. She is **NOT** into beetles, or ants, or worms and is absolutely never playing war because she is too busy being a rock star with Lucy B. Finnegan, who is her best friend (and who I have seen get her finger stuck down a drain hole).

b) She is mostly saying, "Penelope Jones,

it is all your fault, you are such a complete **MORON**," i.e. she is **VERY** irritating.

But this week she is **DOUBLY** irritating and it is all because of the **HORMONES**.

HORMONES are chemicals that are inside you when you are a teenager and make you do things like grow hair in your armpits, and say, "I hate you, you are ruining my life." And no one is allowed to say anything about it except, "It is just her **HORMONES**." Which is not fair, because when I said I hated Bridget Grimes (who is the best student in class and Mr. Schumann's favorite) because she had beaten me at Boggle three times in a row, no one said, "It is just her **HORMONES**," they said, "Penelope Jones, that is a very unkind thing to say."

Mom says the sooner the **TEENAGE YEARS** are all over the better. But Daisy's do not even start for one year, three months and eleven days, so it is a long wait. Anyway, what the **HORMONES** have done now is that they have made Daisy be **IN LOVE**. **IN LOVE** means she is completely wanting to kiss a boy, and that boy is Joshua Bottomley and he sits next to her in French and smells like air freshener and once beat George Helmet at running even though George has the longest legs in sixth

grade and maybe the world. I say he does not sound very **AMAZING** because I do not like air fresheners or French and I bet he can't touch his nose with the tip of his tongue.

But Gran says love is **BLIND**, e.g. Grandpa Jones (who is dead now, but wasn't before) looked a little like an orangutan, and couldn't swim, but she still **LOVED** him.

And Mom says Dad wears wrinkled pants
and drinks orange juice from the carton, even
though she has told him a million times that it
is unhygienic, but she still **LOVES** him.

And Dad is possibly about to say something
about Mom but she makes her lips go thin and so he
changes his mind and says Dr. Cement has eyes like
hard-boiled eggs which is why everyone calls him
Dr. Bugeye, but Mrs. Cement still **LOVES** him. And

I say I hope I am **NEVER** in love, because it is **BLIND** and what if I am in **LOVE** with, e.g. Henry Potts, who is Cosmo's mortal enemy and is always throwing erasers at him; or Brady O'Grady, who has patterns shaved in his hair and a dog called Killer; or Fraser Forks, who does not even go to school and only eats vegetables. And Mom says she hopes not either, because I am enough of a handful as it is. Only **FOR ONCE** I am not as much of a handful as Daisy.

Because what happens is that Daisy is wanting Joshua Bottomley to come to dinner. But because of the **HORMONES** she is also **NOT** wanting a lot of other things, i.e.:

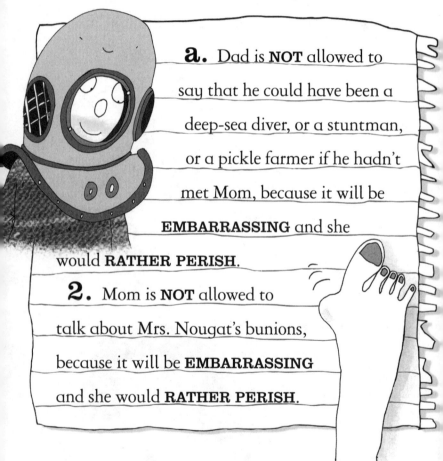

a. Dad is **NOT** allowed to say that he could have been a deep-sea diver, or a stuntman, or a pickle farmer if he hadn't met Mom, because it will be <u>**EMBARRASSING**</u> and she would **RATHER PERISH**.

2. Mom is **NOT** allowed to talk about Mrs. Nougat's bunions, because it will be **EMBARRASSING** and she would **RATHER PERISH**.

3) Gran is **NOT** allowed to let Barry, who is her cat, eat the dinner, because it is **CAT FOOD** and **CAT FOOD ONLY** for Barry, and also it will be **EMBARRASSING** and she would **RATHER PERISH**.

iv. I am **NOT EVEN** allowed in the house, because it will be **EMBARRASSING** and she would **RATHER PERISH**.

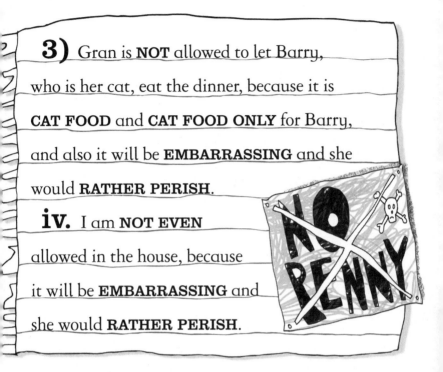

And **AMAZINGLY** Mom says yes to **ALL** of these things, because Gran will be at Arthur Peason's house playing rummy, Dad will be busy solving a crisis to do with some yellow lines on the road, and I will be at Cosmo's eating kale chips. Which I say is not fair because I am not even **INTO** kale chips and also because when I asked if the man who sleeps at the bus shelter could come to dinner, Mom said no he could not. But Mom says it is not the same and anyway, it is Daisy's **HORMONES**.

And I am not in any way happy about Daisy's **HORMONES**, and decide I would very much like to have some **HORMONES** for myself, and so that is when I have my **BRILLIANT IDEA™**, which is to invent some. And so I go to Cosmo's house, because he has a chemistry set **AND** is actually allowed to use it, because of the **FREEDOM** and **SELF-EXPRESSION**. I have a chemistry set but I am **NOT** allowed to use it, although it is not to do with **FREEDOM** and **SELF-EXPRESSION**, it is to do with the time I tried to invent monkeys, and the time I tried to invent gold, and the time I wasn't trying to invent anything but I accidentally invented something that made the house fill with purple smoke and we had to call the fire department.

And Cosmo is also very **INTO** inventing some hormones (although in fact he is **INTO** inventing anything, especially if it is the first-ever time machine made out of a

bus, some tinfoil and an alarm clock – only Mr.
Schumann has told him a million times that
that will **NEVER** happen) and so we get out the
chemistry set and also a lot of things from the
kitchen cabinets, e.g.:

a) Some homemade ginger jam
ii) Some green food coloring that did
not hurt animals when it was being made
c. Some homemade lemonade
4. Some organic chickpea flour
V. Some wheat-free
and sugar-free cookies

The jam and cookies are not to experiment with, they are to eat, because according to Mr. Schumann your brain needs a teaspoon of sugar an hour to work properly, only this does not mean Alexander Pringle is allowed to eat peanut butter and jelly sandwiches in the classroom, it means eating **SENSIBLY**. But Sunflower does not have a lot of sensible food and so it is jam on cookies.

So we are using the kitchen table because that is **SENSIBLE**, and wearing our goggles for **SAFETY**, and Cosmo is wearing his white coat, which is what inventors wear, and I am wearing a silver cape, which is what Captain Danger wears, because it is that or a Jedi outfit.

And we are inventing like **CRAZY**, i.e. we invent:

1. Green stuff

b) Fizzy stuff

3. Green fizzy stuff

But no hormones yet, so we decide to have our snack because it has been quite **ARDUOUS** and our brains might need more sugar, and so we eat eight cookies and eight spoonfuls of jam. And that is when I have my **BRILLIANT IDEA™** Number 2, which is to use the jam for inventing after all, because it is really sticky and also gloopy and I think hormones are definitely sticky or maybe gloopy.

And so what we do is we get the glass beaker
from the chemistry set and in it we put:

1. The jam
2. The flour
c) The lemonade
iv. A cookie that has broken
5. The green food coloring

And it is definitely gloopy, and a little crunchy
as well, so we taste it but it does not taste like

HORMONES, it tastes
like lemon and ginger
and it definitely does
not make me want
to **PERISH**.

And Cosmo says this is because we don't have the **SECRET INGREDIENT** and I say, "What is the **SECRET INGREDIENT**?" and he says he is not sure, and so we look in the cabinets and Cosmo says it is definitely **NOT** brown spaghetti or lentils or tomato juice. And then we look in the fridge and Cosmo says it is definitely **NOT** cheese with holes in it or hummus. So then we look in the bathroom but Sunflower says even though she believes in **FREEDOM** and **SELF-EXPRESSION** she does not believe in eating soap. So then I have my

BRILLIANT IDEA™

Number 3, which is to ask Mrs. Butterworth at the general store, because even though she is always saying stuff like "I have got my beady eye on you" and has a mustache, she has also won the St. Regina's church fair muffin bake-off for two years in a row and it is down to her **SECRET INGREDIENT**.

Only when we get to the general store, Mrs. Butterworth is not completely **INTO** telling me her **SECRET INGREDIENT** because she says I will tell Gran and then Gran will win the muffin bake-off and will walk around with her nose in the air.

And I say Gran does not cook muffins, she does not even cook a boiled egg, she is mostly busy watching *Animal SOS* (which is a TV series where animals are always almost dying but then they don't and it is **MIRACULOUS**).

Plus she does not have her nose in the air because her back is bent and so it is more towards the ground. And Mrs. Butterworth says in that case she **WILL** tell us the **SECRET INGREDIENT**, and it is baking soda. And so we buy some, and Mrs. Butterworth says she will keep her beady eye on us anyway, but we do not mind because we are about to invent **HORMONES**.

And what we do when we get back to
Cosmo's is we add **ALL** of the baking soda to
the glass beaker. And this time something
DOES happen. And it is that the green
jammy stuff begins to foam. And it is not just
a small amount of foam, it is quite largish

and quite fast. And it is foaming all over the
table, and onto the floor, and across the floor,
and out of the door.

And Cosmo says it is definitely **ALIEN
ECTOPLASM**, because he is really **INTO** alien
ectoplasm, but I taste it and it is very strange
and not at all nice any more and I say it is
definitely **HORMONES**. And it is true, because
then I say,

I hate you.

And then Cosmo tastes some
and he says,

No, I hate **YOU**.

And we are **HATING** like **CRAZY** and that is when Sunflower comes in and decides she does not believe in **FREEDOM** and **SELF-EXPRESSION** so much today and that we will both have to have dinner at my house after all. And I say it is **VICTORY NUMBER ONE** for the **HORMONES** and Cosmo agrees and so we put some of the **HORMONES** in the jam jar and go back to my house.

Only Daisy does not think this is a **VICTORY** at all because Joshua Bottomley is going to be here absolutely any minute and me and Cosmo are completely covered in green jam and she will be **EMBARRASSED** and would **RATHER PERISH**. And I say it is not green jam, it is **HORMONES**, and also **I** would **RATHER PERISH**.

And Cosmo says **HE** would **RATHER PERISH**.
Only Mom says she is **UP TO HERE** with all the
PERISHING and to get upstairs and get cleaned
up before she **PERISHES** herself and then **NO
ONE** will have dinner at all, **HORMONES**
or not.

And so we do, because even though we have eaten the cookies and the jam we are pretty tired with all the inventing and our brains definitely need more sugar, and possibly some fish sticks too.

Only when we get back downstairs we are very surprised because a lot of people have appeared from nowhere and Cosmo says maybe someone has invented the first-ever time machine made out of a bus and some tinfoil and an alarm clock, but Mom says no they have not, because that is **NEVER** going to happen. What **HAS** happened is that Gran has had an argument with Arthur Peason about the Jack of Spades and so **SHE** is here. And Dad has amazingly solved the crisis with the yellow lines but then has accidentally set off the fire alarm, so **HE** is here. And I say I hate them all and they have ruined my life. But Daisy says I do not, because **SHE** hates everyone and they have ruined **HER** life because now Joshua Bottomley will not be **IN LOVE** with her.

And for once I am thinking that Daisy is right, because when we

are eating dinner Joshua Bottomley is not looking at all **IN LOVE**, he is looking at Barry, who is eating a bowl of cereal. And also at me and Cosmo, because we are still wearing the white coat and the silver cape with the green jammy stuff on the front. And that is when I have my **BRILLIANT IDEA™** Number 4, which is to give Joshua Bottomley some extra **HORMONES** because then he will absolutely definitely be **IN LOVE**.

And so I am **RACKING MY BRAINS** about
how to give Joshua Bottomley the extra
hormones, because I do not think he will eat
green jam out of a jar, when Dad has one of his

which is a little like a **BRILLIANT IDEA™**
only Mom does not usually agree. And his idea
is to make **SMOOTHIES**, which is when you
mix up a lot of fruit and things and drink it
and it tastes delicious. And I can tell Mom is
about to say something about this because her
lips go thin **AGAIN** and because last time Dad
made smoothies he put Spam in them and
even he had to admit that Spam smoothies are
bad. But Dad says he will not put any Spam

in them, he will just put bananas and milk and strawberries and his **SECRET INGREDIENT** in. Only his **SECRET INGREDIENT** is not the same as Mrs. Butterworth's **SECRET INGREDIENT**, it is **GREEN FOOD COLORING**, because it turns the smoothie into alien ectoplasm. Which is when I have my next

BRILLIANT IDEA™

which is to add the **HORMONES** to Joshua Bottomley's smoothie, because it will be green and he will not be able to tell the difference, and then he will be **IN LOVE** for sure.

And so I am helping Dad like **CRAZY** by
stirring smoothies and Mom says it is nice to see
me being so **HELPFUL**, even if I am in a jammy
cape. And everyone is happy, even Daisy,
because she says her smoothie actually tastes like

fruit this time and that Joshua
Bottomley should definitely try
his. And he does, only Joshua
Bottomley does not think it
tastes like fruit, because he turns

palish and throws up

on the table. And

Gran says maybe he is

allergic to strawberries, because

Mrs. Gibbon is allergic to

strawberries and if she eats

even one her tongue

swells up and she

gets hives on her

thighs and nearly dies. And then

Joshua turns even more palish.

But Daisy says he is not allergic to strawberries because she has seen him eat a strawberry candy and he is not dead. And I say maybe it is not strawberries, it is **HORMONES**.

And Mom says,

WHAT hormones, Penelope Jones?

And I say the ones we invented at Cosmo's house and put in the smoothie to make him fall **IN LOVE**. And that is when Dad does his honking goose laugh. But Mom does not see the funny side, because she says it is very dangerous inventing things and making people drink them without telling them and we must **NEVER** do it again. And nor does Joshua Bottomley, who says can he go home please?

And nor does Daisy, who is definitely **EMBARRASSED** and wanting to **PERISH**. She says,

It is all your fault, Penelope Jones, you are such a **COMPLETE MORON**.

But for once I do not mind, because the next day she decides she is not **IN LOVE** with Joshua Bottomley, she is in love with George Helmet after all. It is her **HORMONES**.

Penny Dreadful

and the
New Girl

Mr. Schumann is our principal

and he is mostly saying things like, "Penelope Jones, I am **SICK AND TIRED** of telling you that chairs are for **SITTING** on, not **DANGLING UPSIDE DOWN** oh,

and if you do not **STOP** the dangling this **INSTANT** I will be **FORCED** to take away a gold star." Even though in actual fact he has already taken away **ALL** my gold stars this week for several things that were completely not my fault, e.g.:

1. Accidentally getting locked in the bathroom because me and Cosmo were testing how super superglue was on the door and it turns out it is very super, which was a scientific experiment and so if you think about it I should **GET** a gold star, not have one taken away.

b) Accidentally getting Luke Bruce's coat stuck on top of the apple tree because we were having a competition to see who had the superpower of throwing, and it is me.

C. Accidentally getting stuck up the apple tree trying to get Luke Bruce's coat back down again, which meant Mr. Schumann had to call the fire department (and they were already unhappy about the time they had to come to school to rescue Gran's cat Barry, who I brought in for show-and-tell and who ran up the curtain in the cafeteria and got stuck).

But I do not tell him this because this week Mr. Schumann is even more **SICK AND TIRED** than usual, because there is a **NEW GIRL** coming to our school and she is named Elsie Maud. Mr. Schumann says Elsie Maud's dad is someone especially **IMPORTANT**, so we must absolutely **SET AN EXAMPLE** and show her we are **KIND** and **SMART** and **CALM**, otherwise she will go to The Greely Academy for Girls like my cousin Georgia May Morton-Jones, which has a swimming pool and Mandarin (which is not a fruit, it is a language).

I say she would be **CRAZY** to go to The Greely Academy for Girls because they have to wear ties and hats, but Mr. Schumann is looking like he thinks it would be good if we wore ties and hats, only possibly not the policeman's hat that

Cosmo Moon Webster

is wearing right now.

Anyway, Mr. Schumann asks us if we can be **TRUSTED** to **SET THE EXAMPLE** and be **KIND** and **CALM** and we all say

Except for Alexander Pringle who cannot say anything because he is eating a peanut butter and jelly sandwich, which Miss Patterson says is definitely **NOT** an example of anything.

And after that everyone is **RACKING THEIR BRAINS** like **CRAZY** to guess who Elsie Maud's **IMPORTANT** dad is, e.g.:

1. Bridget Grimes, who is the best student in the class and Mr. Schumann's favorite, says he is probably Head of Foreign Affairs.

b) Brady O'Grady

(who has had an arrow

shaved into his hair by Shaniqua Reynolds at Hair Today, only he moved and it looks more like a caterpillar) says he is probably Wayne Plane, superstar soccer player, because he is very **BIG** on soccer.

3. Henry Potts, who is Cosmo Moon Webster's mortal enemy, says he is probably Maximus Terror, leader of the Zombiebots, because he is very **BIG** on Maximus Terror.

Only Cosmo is not so big on Maximus Terror so he throws an eraser at Henry Potts and it misses and hits Cherry Scarpelli on the nose, and she starts crying because she cannot be in the Broadley Junior Homecoming Pageant with a bulgy nose.

And then Miss Patterson says we are definitely **NOT SETTING AN EXAMPLE** or being **KIND** or **CALM**. But I say we are being **SMART** because if he **IS** Maximus Terror then we will know we can defeat him with our laser-eyed Dogbots. But Miss Patterson does not agree and says it would be **SMARTER** to get out our math books and work out how long it will take to fill a bucket with water if the water is pouring in at half a gallon every forty seconds.

★ ★ ✦ ✦

Anyway, when I get home I tell Mom and Dad and Daisy all about Elsie Maud and us **SETTING AN EXAMPLE** or she will go to The Greely Academy for Girls even though they have hats and learn Mandarin. And Daisy says she is possibly the daughter of Clint Van Spangle, who is her favorite rock star **EVER** and that I have to get his autograph because then Lucy B. Finnegan will be **INSANE** with jealousy.

Clint Van Spangle

And Dad says she is possibly the daughter of a famous Arctic explorer and that he could have been an Arctic explorer if he had not met Mom. Only Mom says he could not, because he does not like even a **LITTLE** snow. And Aunt Deedee, who has come over to find a sock that belongs to Georgia May Morton-Jones, says if the famous father has any sense he will be sending Elsie Maud to The Greely Academy for Girls by the end of the week anyway, because they have Mandarin, and a swimming pool, and hats, and also they have heard of the word **DISCIPLINE**. And I can tell Mom is about to say in fact Mr. Schumann has also heard of the word **DISCIPLINE** because her lips go a little thinnish, but luckily then Gran puts on *Animal SOS*, and so Aunt Deedee goes home

because Georgia May is only allowed to watch the Math Channel.

Anyway, we are **ALL** watching *Animal SOS* and this week it is all about a pet cow named Hilda who has fallen down a cliff and is almost dead, but then the helicopter rescue unit winches her up to safety in a giant blanket and the vet revives her and so she does not die and it is

MIRACULOUS, which I know because Griff

Hunt, who is the presenter, says so.

And that is when I have my

BRILLIANT IDEA™

which is that in fact Elsie Maud's dad is Griff

Hunt. Only Dad says no, he is sure Elsie

Maud's dad is an Arctic explorer. And Daisy

says if he is not Clint Van Spangle then she

would **RATHER PERISH**. And Mom says she

hopes he is anyone **BUT** Griff Hunt, because

then the whole town will be full of TV people

with their funny glasses and accents and

clothes. But Gran is pleased as punch

because she says if he **IS** Griff Hunt then she

will never have to worry about Barry again,

not even when
he gets stuck
in the washing
machine or eats
wasps, because Griff
Hunt will be able to
revive him and shout, "It's a **MIRACLE**."
And I think Gran is right and so I have
my second

BRILLIANT IDEA™,

which is to be best friends with Elsie Maud.
But I will not tell anyone except for Cosmo,
because otherwise they will all start bringing
in their pets that are almost dying so that they
can be revived and **MIRACULOUS**.

Only when I get to school the next day, a lot of other people are wanting to be best friends with Elsie Maud, e.g.:

1. Bridget Grimes, who has brought her a book about kings and queens.

b) Cherry Scarpelli, who has brought her a tiara with pink jewels in it, and a roller skate.

c) Alexander Pringle, who has brought her a peanut butter sandwich, a cookie shaped like a hippo, and two sausage rolls.

But Miss Patterson says friendship is not about roller skates or books and it is definitely not about cookies shaped like hippos, it is about being **KIND**. And also **CALM**, because Bridget Grimes and Cherry Scarpelli, who normally are completely **INTO** sitting next to each other, both want each other to move so Elsie Maud can sit next to them, and are both crying.

And Alexander Pringle is mad because Brady O'Grady has eaten one of his sausage rolls and so he is chasing Brady around the room with a ruler. And Henry Potts is pretending to be Maximus Terror and is using his deathly shrinking ray on Cosmo Moon Webster, only Cosmo says he is wearing his cape of invisibility (which is actually a silver cape, and he is actually wearing it) and so he cannot be shrunk, and so they are arguing like **CRAZY**, and definitely **NOT SETTING AN EXAMPLE**.

Which is when Mr. Schumann walks in with

Elsie Maud, who has hair that is orange-colored and a lot of freckles.

And I can tell immediately that Mr. Schumann is **SICK AND TIRED**, because his face goes pale, and also because he tells

everyone to **STOP** the **SHENANIGANS** and sit back down in their seats so that he can find Elsie Maud a chair.

And so everyone does sit down and they are sticking their hands up absolutely high and going,

Me, me, Mr. Schumann!

But for once I am completely quiet and still because I am very **MESMERIZED**. Which means I am staring, i.e. at Elsie Maud and her orange hair and freckles, which I think I would like very much, and also I would like the badge on her sweater which is a kitten, which is a pet, which is **CLUE NUMBER 1**, and which means her dad is **DEFINITELY** Griff Hunt.

And then **MIRACULOUSLY** Miss Patterson says,

Penelope Jones is being **CALM** so maybe Elsie Maud can sit next to her.

Because there is an empty chair next to me because Cosmo has sat next to Henry Potts to annoy him by being invisible.

Only Mr. Schumann does not look so **INTO** this idea and he says maybe Bridget Grimes can  trade with me and I can sit with Cherry Scarpelli. But Cherry Scarpelli is not into **THIS** idea and starts crying even more. And also Elsie Maud is not into this idea because she sits right down next to me and Mr. Schumann does **NOT EVEN SAY ANYTHING**.

Anyway, what happens is that I am **PLEASED AS PUNCH** because what we are doing first is **ART** and we are doing **COLLABORATIVE COLLAGES**, which means

WORKING TOGETHER to glue a lot of stuff on a big piece of paper and absolutely **NO ARGUING**. And I say we should do a collage of a cow that is dead and being winched by a helicopter and Elsie Maud says this is a **BRILLIANT** idea, which is **CLUE NUMBER 2**. And so I am cutting out a picture of a cow and gluing it upside down and Elsie Maud is squeezing red paint over it for blood.

Only then Henry Potts decides he needs red paint because him and Cosmo are doing a collage of Maximus Terror fighting some laser-eyed Dogbots, only they are not doing it very **COLLABORATIVELY** because Cosmo is mostly being invisible.

Only Elsie Maud says Maximus Terror does not have blood, he has green ectoplasm, and so Henry needs green paint.

And then there is a lot of arguing and saying, And,

And Henry and Elsie Maud are both squeezing paint all over the Maximus Terror picture and also quite a bit over each other, and some gets on Cherry Scarpelli's and Bridget Grimes's picture, which is of fairies on a rainbow. Only Cherry Scarpelli and Bridget Grimes are not **INTO** the blood **OR** ectoplasm on the fairies and they start crying, which is when Miss Patterson says we have done enough **COLLABORATION** for one day and maybe we should do **NATURE OBSERVATION** instead, which means looking at plants and insects in the playground and collecting things in shoeboxes and **ABSOLUTELY NO PLAYING AROUND ON THE JUNGLE GYM**.

So we are outside, **ABSOLUTELY NOT** playing around on the jungle gym and **ABSOLUTELY** looking at an earwig that is eating an ant, which we put in our nature shoebox. And I say,

And she says,

Maybe your dad could save the ant, Elsie Maud.

It would be **MIRACULOUS** because the ant is very dead.

Which is **CLUE NUMBER 3**. And I am about to do more clues when something very interesting happens, i.e. Cosmo **OBSERVES** some **NATURE** and it is a dead pigeon on the sidewalk behind the railings, which is when I have my next **BRILLIANT IDEA™**, which is to give Elsie Maud the dead pigeon and then her dad can **REVIVE** it, which will be **MIRACULOUS** and also **CLUE NUMBER 4**. And **AMAZINGLY** Elsie Maud agrees and so we are trying to reach the pigeon with a twig when Alexander Pringle says he will reach it for Elsie Maud with his **BARE HANDS**, because he has age-14 size arms and ours are only age-9 size. And Elsie Maud says this is a good idea, but what would be even better is if he also stuck his head through the railings to see what he is doing. And Alexander Pringle says he will do **ANYTHING** for Elsie Maud, even cut off his arm. Which we think might be a good idea for later because it would be very interesting to see a cut-off arm, but right now he can just stick his head through the railings and get the dead pigeon. And amazingly he **CAN** reach the pigeon because of the age-14 size arms, but it turns out his head is also age-14 size because it does not want to come out of the railings as easily as it went in.

And then what happens is that Cosmo says he will save Alexander Pringle with his cape of invisibility and invisible arms. So he is pulling very hard on Alexander Pringle with his invisible arms, but all that is happening is that Alexander Pringle's face is getting very red and he is saying,

a lot, which is when Mr. Schumann comes outside to see what all the **SHENANIGANS** are.

And completely immediately he is **SICK AND TIRED** because he says now he will have to call the fire department **AGAIN**, and also because it is clear we have not been **SETTING AN EXAMPLE** for Elsie Maud or being **KIND** or **CALM**.

And so it will be singing practice for the rest of the day, because if our brains are **BUSY** looking at songbooks and our voices are **BUSY** singing, then we will not be able to be **BUSY** creating **SHENANIGANS**.

And so we sing all afternoon and there are no **SHENANIGANS** except that we are singing a song about clocks and Elsie Maud says she can in fact do the tune by **BURPING**. And she does and it is fantastic and then everyone is burping like **CRAZY**, except for Bridget Grimes, who is still gloomy about the ectoplasm on the fairies, and except for Alexander Pringle who is still stuck in the railings.

Only then Elsie Maud does a really
big burp and a little pink jello comes
back up, which is when
Mr. Schumann comes in with a
tall man with orange hair
and freckles and
who is almost
DEFINITELY
Elsie Maud's
dad and
definitely **NOT**
Griff Hunt.

And the Mr. **NOT**-Griff-Hunt is completely not happy about several things:

1. Because the floor is covered in green and red paint and also pink jello mess, and so is Elsie Maud.

b) Because there is a boy with his head stuck in the railings on the playground.

iii. Because Elsie Maud's **COLLABORATIVE** collage is of a dead cow being winched by a helicopter.

iv. Because Miss Patterson has given him Elsie Maud's nature shoebox and inside is an earwig, an ant and a dead pigeon.

And Mr. Schumann turns very pale and says,

Who is **RESPONSIBLE** for this?

And I am quite **INTO** being

RESPONSIBLE so I say,

I am. Because we thought Elsie Maud's dad was maybe possibly Griff Hunt, who is on *Animal SOS*, which is this TV series where animals almost die and then they don't and it is **MIRACULOUS**. And he is going to revive the pigeon and the ant and shout, "It's a **MIRACLE!**"

Only Elsie Maud's dad says he is not going to revive the ant or the pigeon because he is not Griff Hunt. And he is not a lot of other people either:

a) The Head of Foreign Affairs
b) Wayne Plane
3. Maximus Terror
iv) Clint Van Spangle
5. An Arctic explorer

But he absolutely **IS** important because he is the new priest at St. Regina's church.

★ ☆ ✦ ✭

When I get home I tell everyone about Mr. **NOT**-Griff-Hunt and Dad is absolutely disappointed that he is not an Arctic explorer and Daisy is absolutely disappointed that he is not Clint Van Spangle and Mom is absolutely disappointed that I put a dead pigeon in a box and got Alexander Pringle's head stuck in railings.

Only when I get to school the next day, Alexander Pringle's head is not in the railings anymore and in fact the railings are not there **EITHER** and nor is Elsie Maud, because she has gone to The Greely Academy for Girls after all. Which means Mr. Schumann is very **SICK AND TIRED** to say the least.

But he is not as **SICK AND TIRED** as Aunt Deedee. Because when I get home from school she is calling and is very angry because Georgia May Morton-Jones got her head stuck in some railings, and for once it is completely **NOT MY FAULT**. It is Elsie Maud's.

The End

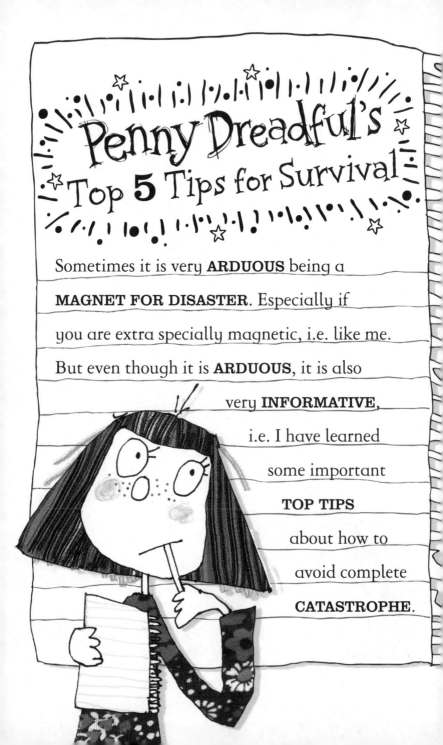

Penny Dreadful's
Top 5 Tips for Survival

Sometimes it is very **ARDUOUS** being a

MAGNET FOR DISASTER. Especially if

you are extra specially magnetic, i.e. like me.

But even though it is **ARDUOUS**, it is also

very **INFORMATIVE**,

i.e. I have learned

some important

TOP TIPS

about how to

avoid complete

CATASTROPHE.

Number 1

Get a DISGUISE

It is completely important not to look like me, i.e. Penelope Jones, when I am being very magnetic, e.g. accidentally knocking over a teetering stack of bean cans at the general store. So sometimes I dress up as Cosmo, i.e. in a Jedi outfit and boots, because it completely confuses Mrs. Butterworth's beady eye and however hard she **RACKS** her brain she is **DISCOMBOBULATED** as to who to shout at.

Another good disguise is dressing up as a burglar, because burglars wear balaclavas which **COMPLETELY** cover up their face. Although it is possible you would get shouted at for being a burglar anyway.

Number 2
Collect COLLATERAL, i.e. money

Coins are **EVERYWHERE**, e.g. on the ground outside the general store, down the back of the sofa and mostly in Dad's pants pocket.

Collect them **ALL** because you never know

when you might need them for:

1. Paying people back, e.g. your Aunt Deedee

when you have accidentally broken a glass

vase or called Russia for instance.

b) Buying essential supplies

like cookies or licorice sticks.

iii. Playing ludo, because you have

used the actual plastic counters to

flick at your mortal enemy.

Number 3
Be PREPARED for EVERY EVENTUALITY

DISASTERS are **EVERYWHERE** and you never

know when you might be super-magnetic,

so it is completely important to have a box

of useful things for **EVERY EVENTUALITY**,

i.e. anything, e.g.:

a) **COLLATERAL** (see above).

2. **A DISGUISE** (see above).

3. Cookies (for **ARDUOUS**

JOURNEYS).

4. A bottle of dishwashing liquid and a

sponge (for when you have spilled something, or

accidentally drawn some Roman soldiers

marching along the kitchen wall).

e) A flashlight (for when you have

accidentally blown up the vacuum cleaner by

trying to suck up the dishwashing liquid, and

all the lights have gone off).

Number 4

Find a TRUSTY SCAPEGOAT

This means someone else to **BLAME**, e.g. in our house everyone mostly blames me, even though it is not usually my fault, it is that I am a **MAGNET FOR DISASTER**. So I usually blame Barry the cat, because he is most often eating things that are **NOT** cat food. E.g. when Daisy said, "Where is my last chocolate-covered cherry, Penelope Jones? I **KNOW** it is you who has eaten it," I said, "But in fact maybe it is not I, it is **BARRY**, because he completely **ADORES** cherries and chocolate, so ha!"

Number 5

Get a FAITHFUL FRIEND

If you are very magnetic like me, it is
COMPLETELY important to have a faithful
friend, which is not the same thing as a
scapegoat, and is also not the same as a dog
(especially not one that isn't yours but which
you have found outside the general store only it
is not lost at all), but e.g. Cosmo Moon
Webster. Because faithful friends will always
stand up for you, even when you have
accidentally exploded pudding in
their microwave, and
even if they are a boy
and exactly a week
older than you.

My
Faithful Friend

Everybody Loves Penny!

"Penny is an exciting and entertaining character who always has **BRILLIANT IDEAS**... If Penny was my **BFF** then life would never be dull."

Rachel, age 9

"Penny Dreadful stories are very funny and exciting. It is a fantastic series."

Polly, age 10

"I liked Penny because she's naughty, but in a way she's also funny too! I did not like Mrs. Butterworth because she's got a mustache."

Millie, age 8

"I think Penny Dreadful is, well, dreadfully funny. (She sounds like my brother — hee hee.) PS I'm turning a little dreadful too."

Islay, age 8

"I think Penny Dreadful is a great book! I learned 'e.g.' means 'for example'. I learned 'i.e.' means 'that is'."

Bryn, age 8

"A hilariously funny read!"

Anastasia, age 11

"I loved Penny Dreadful, especially in **'PENNY DREADFUL BECOMES A HAIRDRESSER'**. And the lady with the mustache. Fantastico!"

Leila, age 7

"I love Penny Dreadful, she is brilliant and very funny."

Iona, age 6

"I wanted to read on and on and on...it was <u>soooo</u> good."

Matt, age 8

"This book is funny and full of **BRILLIANT IDEAS** and I like the way it uses '**E.G.**' all the time!"

Megan Emily, age 6

"Here are some of the things I enjoyed about the book:

1. I liked it when Penny and Cosmo tried to shave Barry the cat (the coolest cat ever).
b) Does Penny ever comb her hair?
3. Where did Cosmo get his Jedi suit... I want one!
iv. I liked Mrs. Butterworth at the general store and her mustache!"

Gruffudd, age 10

Joanna Nadin

wrote this book –
and lots of others
like it. She is small,
funny, clever,
sneaky and musical.
Before she became a writer, she wanted to be a
champion ballroom dancer or a jockey, but she
was actually a lifeguard at a swimming pool,
a radio newsreader, a cleaner in an old people's
home, and a juggler. She likes peanut butter on
toast for breakfast, and jam on toast for dessert.
Her perfect day would involve baking, surfing,
sitting in cafes in Paris, and playing with
her daughter – who reminds her a lot
of Penny Dreadful…

Jess Mikhail

illustrated this book.
She loves creating funny
characters with bright
colors and fancy

patterns to make people smile.
Her favorite place is her tiny home, where she
lives with her tiny dog and spends lots of time
drawing, scanning, scribbling, printing, stamping,
and sometimes using her scary computer. She
loves to rummage through a good charity shop to
find weird and wonderful things. A
perfect day for her would have to
involve a sunny beach and large
amounts of spicy foods and ice
cream (not together).

For Joseph Walter and Elsie Maud, who do,
occasionally, cause a kerfuffle, but it is
almost always never their fault,
and absolutely a **GOOD THING**.

First published in the UK in 2012 by Usborne Publishing Ltd., Usborne House,
83-85 Saffron Hill, London EC1N 8RT, England. www.usborne.com

Copyright © Joanna Nadin, 2012
Illustrations copyright © Usborne Publishing Ltd., 2012

The right of Joanna Nadin to be identified as the author of this work has been asserted by her in
accordance with the Copyright, Designs and Patents Act, 1988.

The name Usborne and the devices 🏆 🎈 are Trade Marks of Usborne Publishing Ltd.

A CIP catalogue record for this book is available from the British Library.

First published in America in 2014 AE.

PB ISBN 9780794523053
ALB ISBN 9781601303394
JFMAMJJ SOND/17 00841/21
Printed in China.